DALE JARRETT

IN THE FAST LANE

David and Patricia Armentrout

Publishing LLC
Vero Beach, Florida 32964

© 2007 Rourke Publishing LLC

All rights reserved. No part of this book may be reproduced or utilized in any form or by any means, electronic or mechanical including photocopying, recording, or by any information storage and retrieval system without permission in writing from the publisher.

www.rourkepublishing.com

PHOTO CREDITS: Title pg. ©Autostock; all other photos ©Getty Images

Title page: *Dale Jarrett finished 10th at the 2006 Daytona 500.*

Editor: Robert Stengard-Olliges

Cover design by Nicola Stratford

Library of Congress Cataloging-in-Publication Data

Armentrout, David, 1962-
 Dale Jarrett : in the fast lane / David and Patricia Armentrout.
   p. cm. -- (In the fast lane)
 Includes index.
 ISBN 1-60044-216-1 (hardcover)
 ISBN 978-1-60044-309-1 (paperback)
 1. Jarrett, Dale, 1956---Juvenile literature. 2. Automobile racing drivers--United States--Biography--Juvenile literature. I. Armentrout, Patricia, 1960- II. Title. III. Series.
  GV1032.J37A76 2007
  796.72092--dc22
                                2006010781

Printed in the USA

CG/CG

www.rourkepublishing.com – sales@rourkepublishing.com
Post Office Box 3328, Vero Beach, FL 32964

TABLE OF CONTENTS

The Road to Success	4
Like Father, Like Son	6
Grand Nationals	9
Victory Lane At Last	10
Dale vs. Dale	13
Speeding Along	14
Struggles are Worth the Rewards	18
Car and Crew	21
On and Off the Track	22
Glossary	23
Index	24
Further Reading/Websites to Visit	24

THE ROAD TO SUCCESS

For most racecar drivers, the road to success is long and hard. Dale Jarrett's journey was no exception. Dale began his racing career in 1977. Over the years, he learned plenty about stock car racing, while hitting a few speed bumps along the way. But it was Dale's strong will and determination that led him to victory lane.

Born: November 26, 1956
Organization: NASCAR
Car: Ford #88
Car Owner: Robert Yates
Team: Robert Yates Racing
Sponsor: UPS

Dale and Tony Stewart lead the pack at Talladega.

LIKE FATHER, LIKE SON

Stock car racing is a tough career to enter unless you have a lot of money, or you know someone in the business. It makes sense then, that you see a lot of father-son drivers in **NASCAR**.

Dale Jarrett is the son of Hall of Fame driver Ned Jarrett. He practically grew up at the track, where his father raced legends like Richard Petty and Parnelli Jones. As a child, high speed and excitement at the track surrounded Dale, but he didn't consider racing until he was 20 years old.

Dale and his father, racing legend Ned Jarrett.

GRAND NATIONALS

NASCAR's Grand National **series** (now Busch series) **debuted** in 1982. Dale raced 28 of 29 Grand National events that year. He placed in the top ten 14 times and finished sixth in points.

Dale continued to race well for the next three seasons. He finished each year in the top five in points, but still had not won a race.

Dale Jarrett and Michael Waltrip crash during the UAW-GM Quality 500 on October 15, 2005.

Victory Lane at Last

Dale's first NASCAR win was in 1986, almost ten years after his racing career began. It happened at Orange County Speedway, a short track in North Carolina. His winnings totaled $4,750.

Dale entered NASCAR's Winston Cup series (now Nextel Cup) in 1984. By 1990, Dale's skills on the track earned him a spot driving for the oldest team in NASCAR, the Wood Brothers. The following year Dale got his first Winston Cup win racing in the Champion 400 at Michigan International Speedway.

Dale Jarrett has been a fan favorite since he joined the ranks of NASCAR.

DALE VS. DALE

NASCAR opens each Nextel season with its most famous race, the Daytona 500. Dale's first Daytona 500 was in 1988. His first Daytona 500 win was in 1993, and it was a memorable ride. There were 38 lead changes in the 200-lap race. During the final lap, Dale found himself out in front and racing side-by-side with #3 Dale Earnhardt. Earnhardt tried to pass Dale in the final stretch, but it was Jarrett who took the **checkered flag**, just 0.16 seconds (sixteen hundredths of a second) ahead of Earnhardt.

Jarrett leading Earnhardt during the 1993 Daytona 500.

SPEEDING ALONG

Dale didn't win another Winston race in 1993, and raced only Busch events in 1994. Later, he added two more Daytona 500 victories to his list of accomplishments. The first was in 1996, which paid $360,775. The second was in 2000, which paid $2,277,975.

FAST FACTS

Superspeedway- an oval track at least 2 miles long. The longest is the 2.66-mile Talladega Superspeedway in Talladega, Alabama.
Speedway- an oval track between 1 and 2 miles long. The 1.5-mile Homestead-Miami Speedway hosts the last race of the season for both the Busch and Nextel Cup series.
Short track- an oval track less than 1 mile long. The shortest is the 0.526-mile Martinsville Speedway in Martinsville, Virginia.
Road Course- tracks with left and right twists and turns. Currently there are two Nextel races on road courses.

Dale celebrates after winning the 1993 Daytona 500.

FAST FACTS

NASCAR Point System for Each Race

Winner	driver earns 180 points
Runner-up	driver earns 170 points
3rd-6th position	points drop in 5-point increments (3rd position-165 points, 4th-160, 5th-155, and 6th-150 points)
7th-11th position	points drop in 4-point increments
12th-42nd position	points drop in 3-point increments
Last place	driver earns 34 points

Drivers can earn bonus points for leading a lap and leading the most laps

A bird's eye view of Jarrett's pit crew in action at the 2000 Daytona 500.

STRUGGLES ARE WORTH THE REWARDS

Winning the **championship** is not easy. It means continuously earning the big points throughout the racing season. Dale won the NASCAR Winston Cup championship in 1999. He said the reward was worth all the struggles he had along the way.

FAST FACTS

NASCAR began its 2004 season with a new Cup sponsor—Nextel Communications. NASCAR also began a new system for crowning the Cup champion, called 'NASCAR's Chase for the Nextel Cup.' The Chase consists of the final ten races of the 36-race schedule. The top ten drivers in the point standings from the first 26 races, and any driver within 400 points of the leader, are eligible for the prize.

Dale hugs his wife Kelley after winning the NASCAR Cup Championship in 1999.

CAR AND CREW

Winning a race, not to mention the championship, takes teamwork. The #88 Yates racing team includes a crew of mechanics and specialists who maintain the car before, during, and after each race. A pit crew concentrates on servicing #88 during a race, and getting it back on track in a matter of seconds.

Dale's Ford has had many different paint schemes since UPS began sponsorship in 2001. The 2006 car features a new make, the Ford Fusion, and displays more color on top of the car's base white paint.

The #88 team celebrates a win at the Talladega Speedway in 2005.

ON AND OFF THE TRACK

Dale still spends long hours on the track, improving his racing skills. He and his team hope to deliver another championship season.

Off the track, Dale loves spending time with his family. Dale is married and has three children with his wife Kelley, and a son from a previous marriage.

Career Highlights

2005: Placed in the top-ten seven times and finished 15th in points
2004: Placed in the top-ten 14 times and finished 15th in points
2003: Won one Winston Cup race and finished 26th in points
2002: Won two Winston Cup races and finished ninth in points
2001: Won four Winston Cup races and finished fifth in points
2000: Won two Winston Cup races including the Daytona 500, and finished fourth in points
1999: Winston Cup champion

GLOSSARY

championship — (CHAM pee uhn ship) each driver is awarded points in a race, with winners earning the most. The driver with the most points at the end of a season wins the championship.

debuted — (day BYOOD) occurred for the first time

checkered flag — (CHEK erd flag) a black and white checked banner waved by a race official. The first driver to receive the flag wins the race.

NASCAR — National Association for Stock Car Auto Racing: the governing body for the Nextel Cup, Craftsman Truck, and Busch series, among others

series — (SIHR eez) a group of races that make up one season

INDEX

Busch series   9, 14
Daytona 500   13, 14, 22
Earnhardt, Dale   13
Grand National series   9
Jarrett, Ned   6
Jones, Parnelli   6
NASCAR points explained   16
Nextel Chase explained   18
Petty, Richard   6
UPS   21
Winston Cup series   10, 14, 18, 22

FURTHER READING

Gigliotti, Jim. *Dale Jarrett: It was Worth the Wait.* Tradition Books, 2003.
Schaefer, A. R. *The Daytona 500.* Capstone Press, 2004.
Buckley, James. *Speedway Superstars.* NASCAR and Reader's Digest, 2004.

WEBSITES TO VISIT

www.nascar.com
www.dalejarrett.com/dale.asp
www.racing.ups.com

ABOUT THE AUTHORS

David and Patricia Armentrout have written many nonfiction books for young readers. They have had several books published for primary school reading. The Armentrouts live in Cincinnati, Ohio, with their two children.